For Mary T – J.W.

UNIVERSITY OF CHICHESTER

CR
P
WIL

MISERY MOO

Jeanne
Willis

and

Tony
Ross

Andersen Press
London

Once upon a time, there was a miserable old cow.
"What's up with you, Misery Moo?" said a little lamb.
"It's raining," moaned the cow.
"Rain makes the grass grow," said the lamb.

"You like grass. Be happy."
It rained and the cow ate the grass.
But the next time the lamb saw her . . .

. . . she was still miserable.

"What's up with you, Misery Moo?" said the lamb.

"It's my birthday. Another year older," moaned the cow.

"Birthdays are fun!" said the lamb. "Let's party! Be happy!"

It was a good party.
But the next time the lamb saw her,
the cow was as miserable as ever.
"What's up with you, Misery Moo?" said the lamb.

"Same old view," moaned the Cow.
"Try looking at it this way," said the lamb. "Just for a laugh . . ."

. . . And he stood on his head!
The cow stood on her head and the view was very funny .
But the next time the lamb saw her . . .

. . . she was as miserable as could be.

"What's up with you, Misery Moo?" said the lamb.

"It's winter," moaned the cow.

"Winter means Christmas," said the lamb. "Happy Christmas!"

They spent Christmas together.
But the cow was so miserable,
she couldn't see the happiness in anything . . .

The fairy lights were too bright. The crackers were too loud.

Father Christmas was too jolly.

The little lamb went home and burst into tears.
Until he met the cow, he had never realised what
a terrible, miserable, rotten old world it was.
No wonder it was impossible to cheer her up!

He couldn't bear to see his friend so sad,
so he decided never to see her again.

Soon, the cow began to miss the lamb's happy face,
and went to look for him.

To her surprise, he was sitting in a muddy puddle,
looking very unhappy indeed.

"What's up with you, Lamby Poo?" she said.
"It's my birthday," sobbed the lamb.
"Birthdays are fun - be happy!" said the cow.
"That's what you said to *me*."

"I know," said the lamb. "But I can't be happy when you're not happy."
"Really?" said the cow. "I never knew you cared!"
"Of course I do!" said the lamb. "When you're sad, I'm sad.
That's how it is with friends."

The cow was so pleased to have a friend,
the last thing she wanted to do was make him sad.
So she gave him the best birthday present ever . . .

the biggest, sunniest smile in the whole, wide, wonderful world.
"You make me soooooooo happy!" said the cow.

The little lamb jumped for joy.

"I love you too, you silly old moo!" he said.
And they lived happily ever after . . .

Even when it rained.